APR 0 2 2005

W9-DDM-779

WITHDRAWN FROM LIBRARY

THE NBA LIBRARY

ABOVE THE RIM

ATLANTIC DIVISION

BY JIM GIGLIOTTI

THE BOSTON CELTICS
THE MIAMI HEAT
THE NEW JERSEY NETS
THE NEW YORK KNICKS
THE ORLANDO MAGIC
THE PHILADELPHIA 76ERS
THE WASHINGTON WIZARDS

Note to readers:

At press time, the NBA was considering a plan that would reorganize the league into six divisions of five teams, beginning in the 2004-05 season. It will also add a 30th team, the Charlotte Bobcats.

THE ATLANTIC DIVISION: The Boston Celtics, the Miami Heat, the New Jersey Nets, the New York Knicks, the Orlando Magic, the Philadelphia 76ers, and the Washington Wizards

Published in the United States of America by The Child's World®
PO Box 326 • Chanhassen, MN 55317-0326 • 800-599-READ • www.childsworld.com

ACKNOWLEDGEMENTS:
The Child's World®: Mary Berendes, Publishing Director

Editorial Directions, Inc.: E. Russell Primm, Editorial Director and Line Editor; Katie Marsico, Assistant Editor; Matthew Messbarger, Editorial Assistant; Susan Hindman, Copy Editor; Melissa McDaniel, Proofreader; Tim Griffin, Indexer; Kevin Cunningham, Fact Checker; James Buckley Jr., Photo Reseacher and Photo Selector

The Design Lab: Kathleen Petelinsek, Designer and Production Artist

PHOTOS:
Cover: Reuters New Media/Corbis
AP/Wide World: 15, 16, 20, 21, 28, 31, 35, 41.
Bettman/Corbis: 7, 8, 9, 10, 18, 19, 23, 24, 25, 33, 34, 38, 39, 40, 44.
Sports Gallery: 13, 14, 26, 29, 30.

Copyright © 2004 by The Child's World®. All rights reserved. No part of the book may be reproduced or utilized in any form or by any means without written permission from the publisher.

LIBRARY OF CONGRESS CATALOGING-IN-PUBLICATION DATA
Gigliotti, Jim.
The Atlantic Division : the Boston Celtics, the Miami Heat, the New Jersey Nets, the New York Knicks, the Orlando Magic, the Philadelphia 76ers, and the Washington Wizards / by Jim Gigliotti.
    p. cm. — (Above the rim)
Summary: Describes the seven teams that make up the Atlantic Division of the National Basketball Association, their histories, famous players, and statistics.
Includes bibliographical references and index.
  ISBN 1-59296-192-4 (lib. bdg. : alk. paper)
1. National Basketball Association—History—Juvenile literature. 2. Basketball—East (U.S.)—History—Juvenile literature. [1. National Basketball Association—History. 2. Basketball.] I. Title. II. Series.
GV885.515.N37A85 2004
796.323'64'0973—dc22
                        2003020032

Every sport has one legendary team. In baseball's major leagues, it's the New York Yankees. In the National Football League, it's the Green Bay Packers. In the National Hockey League, it's the Montreal Canadians (though they spell it Canadiens). They are the **flagship** franchises for each league, the ones that hang the most championship banners and the ones with the most historically interesting tradition and widespread following. In the National Basketball Association (NBA), that club is the Boston Celtics (sorry, Lakers fans).

Through the 2002–03 season, the Celtics had won a record 16 NBA titles, 22 division titles (and tied for two more), and 2,656 games. But it's not just the numbers. It's coach Red Auerbach and his victory cigar . . . Bob Cousy's behind-the-back passes . . . Bill Russell's rebounding and shot-blocking . . . John Havlicek's steals . . . Larry Bird's jumpers . . . even the grinning leprechaun mascot. They're all a big part of the NBA story.

The Celtics' presence alone would make the NBA's Atlantic Division steeped in history, because the team has been around for more than 50 years. But the division's tradition doesn't begin and end in Boston. Two other Atlantic Division franchises, the New York Knicks and the Philadelphia 76ers (originally the Syracuse Nationals), have been around since the beginning of the NBA. They were all playing when the new National Basketball Association was created following the unification of the Basketball Association of America (BAA) and the National Basketball League (NBL) in 1949–1950.

For two decades, those teams played in the NBA's Eastern Division.

In 1970–71, the league expanded to 17 teams, and the Atlantic Division was born. The historic trio was joined that year by the expansion Buffalo Braves.

Since then, the division has undergone a few changes. When the New Jersey Nets entered the NBA in 1976–77 (they were still called the New York Nets at the time), they joined the Atlantic Division. Two years later, Buffalo moved to San Diego to become the Clippers (they're now in Los Angeles and the Pacific Division) and the Washington Bullets moved from the Central Division to the more geographically appropriate Atlantic. The Charlotte Hornets played its expansion year in the Atlantic and its second year in the Midwest Division, before moving to the Central in its third year. Expansion teams Miami and Orlando each played one season in the Western Conference before settling in the Atlantic. Since the 1991–92 season, the division has remained unchanged.

While Boston has the NBA's most storied tradition, the Celtics don't have exclusive rights to NBA lore. Read on, and you'll learn the rich traditions of the other established franchises in the Atlantic Division—and how the newer franchises in Miami and Orlando are building their own histories.

TEAM	YEAR FOUNDED	HOME ARENA	YEAR ARENA OPENED	TEAM COLORS
BOSTON CELTICS	1946	FLEET CENTER	1995	GREEN & WHITE
MIAMI HEAT	1988	AMERICAN AIRLINES ARENA	1999	RED, ORANGE & BLACK
NEW JERSEY NETS	1967	MEADOWLANDS ARENA	1981	GREY, RED, & WHITE
NEW YORK KNICKS	1946	MADISON SQUARE GARDEN	1968	RED, BLUE, & BLACK
ORLANDO MAGIC	1989	TD WATERHOUSE CENTRE	1989	SILVER, TEAL, & PURPLE
PHILADELPHIA 76ERS	1949	CONSECO FIELDHOUSE	2002	RED, WHITE, & BLUE
WASHINGTON WIZARDS	1961	MCI CENTER	1997	BLUE, TEAL, BLACK, & WHITE

THE BOSTON CELTICS

The Celtics were founded as charter members of the BAA in 1946. Their first coach was John (Honey) Russell, and they made the **playoffs** in only their second season, in 1947–48. But to Boston fans, the real history of the Celtics began in 1950. That was the year the club laid the groundwork that made it the most dominant franchise in basketball history.

In 1950, the Celtics hired Red Auerbach as coach. Auerbach quickly found a center in Ed Macauley, who had played for the **defunct** Saint Louis Bombers the previous year. Then, the Celtics got a little lucky. After the Chicago Stags folded, Boston, New York, and Philadelphia drew names of the Stags' three guards out of a hat. The Celtics drew rookie Bob Cousy. At the time, he was the least-desirable choice of the three. Eventually, Cousy made it into the Hall of Fame.

After finishing in last place in the Eastern Division in 1949–50, the Celtics made the playoffs

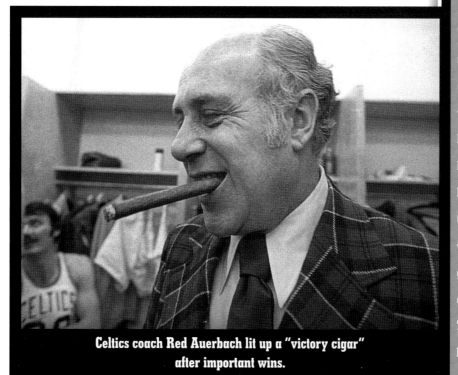

Celtics coach Red Auerbach lit up a "victory cigar" after important wins.

The first home game in Celtics history (November 5, 1946) was delayed an hour by pro basketball's first broken backboard. Boston's Chuck Connors—who went on to greater fame as an actor on television's *The Rifleman*—broke the backboard while dunking warm-up shots.

in 1950–51. Auerbach continued to add pieces to the championship puzzle, including shooting guard Bill Sharman in 1951–52 and Frank Ramsey, the NBA's first true **sixth man,** in 1954–55. Boston won its first postseason series in 1952–53 and reached the playoffs each season through 1955–56, but bowed out every year before the finals.

The big breakthrough came in 1956–57. First, the Celtics selected Holy Cross's Tom Heinsohn in the draft. The team then traded Macauley and

The Celtics played their home games at Boston Garden from the inception of the franchise in 1946–47 through the 1994–95 season. They moved into the new Fleet Center in 1995–96.

The Celtics helped integrate pro basketball in 1950, when they made Duquesne's Charles Cooper the first African-American ever selected in the league draft.

Bob Cousy helped invent the position of point guard in the NBA.

rookie Cliff Hagen to Saint Louis in exchange for center Bill Russell.

After signing Heinsohn and Russell, everything fell into place. Heinsohn was a solid forward and the NBA's Rookie of the Year in 1956–57. Russell was a dominant defensive player and rebounder, who went on to win five NBA Most Valuable Player (MVP) awards. Over the next 13 seasons, the Celtics ruled the NBA like no other team before or since.

Boston won its first championship in 1956–57 with a thrilling 125–123 victory over the Saint Louis Hawks in double overtime in Game 7 of the **NBA Finals.** Saint Louis avenged that defeat in

Bill Russell (No. 6) was the dominant defensive player of the 1960s.

The Celtics beat the Phoenix Suns in one of the greatest games in NBA history in the 1976 finals. With the series tied 2–2, Boston won the pivotal fifth game 128–126 in three overtimes.

1958, but the Celtics bounced back in 1958–59 to win the first of an unprecedented eight consecutive championships.

Over the years, the names of the players changed, but the Celtics maintained a legacy of success. Cousy retired after the club's fifth consecutive title in 1962–63, but John Havlicek arrived the same season. Auerbach stepped down as coach after the eighth straight title in 1965–66. He handed the reins to Russell, who retired as player-coach following the second of back-to-back titles in

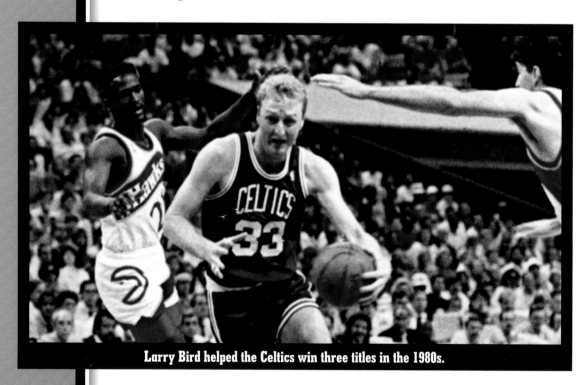

Larry Bird helped the Celtics win three titles in the 1980s.

1968–69. (An important historical note is that when he was named to replace Auerbach, Russell became the first African-American coach of any major professional sports team.)

Center Dave Cowens helped the team win a pair of titles in the 1970s, while the 1980s belonged to Larry Bird. A three-time league MVP, Bird teamed with Robert Parish and Kevin McHale to lead Boston to three more championships.

After winning their 16th title in 1985–86 and losing the 1986–87 finals, the Celtics fell on hard times. The aging club was able to make the playoffs for several seasons after that but did not challenge for a title. Bird retired before the 1992–93 season, and Boston missed the playoffs the following year. In 1996–97, the Celtics fortunes reached their **nadir,** when the club's 15–67 record was the worst in its history.

The next season, however, Rick Pitino was hired as coach and began rebuilding the club. Paul Pierce arrived as a heralded rookie in 1998–99. By 2001–02, he was one of the top players in the NBA, and the Celtics were back in the postseason.

John Havlicek was drafted by the NFL's Cleveland Browns in 1962. He was cut in training camp that year, which turned out to be good for Havlicek's career. He went on to earn 13 All-Star selections during his 16 years in the NBA.

THE MIAMI HEAT

The Heat had an **inauspicious** start as an expansion team in the late 1980s. By the 1990s, however, they had emerged as perennial playoff contenders. The Heat's surge to the top of the Atlantic Division coincided with the arrival of Pat Riley as the club's president and head coach in 1995.

Miami, which joined the league in 1988–89, began play under coach Ron Rothstein as a member of the Midwest Division. Like most expansion teams, the club struggled early. The Heat, however, took a first-year team's troubles to new heights—or depths. Miami set an NBA record by losing its first 17 games. They finally ended the drought with an 89–88 victory over the Los Angeles Clippers for the team's first win.

The Heat won only 15 games that first season. They shifted divisions the next year, joining the Atlantic. The change did little good, as Miami won only 18 games in 1989–90. The addition of rookie

Glen Rice to a roster of returning players such as center Rony Seikaly and forward Grant Long would bode well for the future, however.

By 1991–92, the Heat were in the playoffs, albeit with a losing record (38–44), and they were bounced in the first round by the Chicago Bulls. Two years later, Miami posted its first winning season (42–40) but fell to the Hawks in the first round of the playoffs.

Riley was hired before the 1995–96 season. He had forged his coaching reputation by winning four

The Heat won 14 consecutive road games in 1996–97. It was the third-longest winning streak away from home in NBA history.

Rony Seikaly, a native of Lebanon, led the Heat to the 1992 NBA playoffs.

Pat Riley won the
1,000th game of his
coaching career
when the Heat
began the 2000–01
season by beating
the Orlando Magic.
Riley was only the
second NBA coach
with 1,000 victories
after Lenny Wilkens.

Alonzo Mourning was a dominating defensive player for the Heat.

Glen Rice set a club
record when he
scored 56 points in a
victory over the
Orlando Magic on
April 15, 1995.

NBA titles in Los Angeles. Riley had never missed the playoffs in 13 seasons with the Lakers and the New York Knicks. That streak surely figured to end when he took over a Miami team that went just 32–50 in 1994–95.

Instead, the string continued. A series of off-season moves had brought in the likes of center Alonzo Mourning and guard Tim Hardaway, while shipping out Rice. Mourning led the team in scoring and rebounding while playing a tenacious defense. Tough defense was a big part of Riley's teams.

Miami reached the playoffs in each of Riley's first six seasons, giving the coach an NBA-record 19 teams in the playoffs. The highlight came in

Tim Hardaway was a driving force for Miami.

Former Heat coach Pat Riley directs his team from the bench.

The Heat's first-ever draft pick was Syracuse center Rony Seikaly in 1988.

1996–97, when the Heat posted a franchise-record 61 victories, won the first of four consecutive Atlantic Division titles, and advanced to the Eastern Finals, before losing to Chicago.

The Heat could not build on that success in the ensuing seasons, however, and in 2001–02 missed the playoffs for the first time under Riley. The club was 25–57 the next year, and Riley handed over the coaching reins to Stan Van Gundy before the 2003–04 season.

CHAPTER 3

THE NEW JERSEY NETS

The Nets' brief history has been a roller-coaster ride of dizzying heights, stunning drops, and twists and turns. The franchise began play in the American Basketball Association (ABA) in 1967. That fledgling league wanted a team in New York, the nation's marquee city. Instead, it got a squad of journeymen and **semipros** who played in a converted **armory** in Teaneck, New Jersey, and went by the name the New Jersey Americans.

The next year, the club changed its name to the New York Nets and moved to Commack Arena on Long Island. Thus began a series of **nomadic** adventures that took the team to five different arenas before finally settling in New Jersey—and taking the name New Jersey Nets—in 1977.

The original Americans won 36 games, but by the next year the team was the ABA's worst at 17–61. The Nets acquired their first star in 1970, when they signed flashy, high-scoring forward Rick Barry. One

The Americans tied the Kentucky Colonels for the final postseason spot in the ABA's inaugural season, forcing a one-game playoff at Commack Arena on Long Island. When the teams arrived, however, they found the court in unplayable condition, and Kentucky won by forfeit.

High-scoring Rick Barry was a star on early Nets' teams.

year later, the team was in the ABA Finals. Though they lost that series to the Indiana Pacers, they won fans and exposure in New York City.

Barry was gone the next year, and the club quickly fell among the league also-rans again. But the Nets replaced Barry's star power and scoring ability before the 1973–74 season by acquiring Julius "Dr. J." Erving. His dazzling array of skills produced a league-best 27.4 points per game. The Nets waltzed to the ABA title in his first year with the club. Two years later, the Nets won the last ABA championship.

High-flying "Dr. J" slam-dunked the Nets to two ABA titles.

The Americans changed their name to the Nets in 1968 to rhyme with two of New York's other teams, the Mets and the Jets. It originally was a whimsical suggestion by a local sportswriter.

The Nets (along with several other ABA teams) joined the NBA in 1976, but their fortunes plummeted again as quickly as they had risen. Erving was traded to the 76ers before the season began, and the Nets finished a league-worst 22–60. Over the next quarter-century, the team had some good players—including Buck Williams, the team's all-time leading scorer and rebounder, and the popular Drazen Petrovic, who was tragically killed at age 28 in a car accident in 1993. Still, the Nets managed

The Nets won the last ABA title by rallying from a 22-point deficit against Denver in Game Six of the Finals to win 112–106.

Kenyon "K-Mart" Martin urges Nets' fans to cheer louder!

only seven winning seasons.

Finally, in 2001–02, the Nets had their best NBA season. Newly acquired point guard Jason Kidd and young forward Kenyon Martin led coach Byron Scott's team to a 52–30 record and the Atlantic Division title. The Nets beat Indiana, Charlotte, and Boston in the playoffs before Los Angeles ended their run in the NBA Finals.

Jason Kidd's passing was a key part of the Nets' two NBA Finals trips.

Undaunted by that defeat, New Jersey won 49 games in 2002–03 and again reached the NBA Finals. The Nets played well, but lost in six games to the San Antonio Spurs. Even with the two straight Finals losses, the Nets' roller coaster was clearly back near the top again.

Nets coach Byron Scott was a member of three NBA-championship teams while playing with the Los Angeles Lakers.

CHAPTER 4

THE NEW YORK KNICKS

When the New York Knicks earned the first pick in the 1985 NBA draft, the club and its fans felt as if they'd won the lottery. Actually, the Knicks had won the lottery—the first NBA draft lottery. (Before 1985, only the poorest teams qualified for the top pick; now, every team that misses the playoffs has a chance. All these teams enter a drawing to determine the draft order.) And, as everyone knew, the first pick in the 1985 draft would be coveted center Patrick Ewing from Georgetown.

The Knicks did indeed take Ewing in the draft, and his selection helped usher in the longest sustained streak of excellence in club history: 14 consecutive playoff appearances from 1988 to 2001, three division titles, and two Eastern Conference championships. And yet, the big prize—an NBA championship—eluded the Knicks during all those years. That's an old story for New York. One of the most successful franchises since joining the

Joe Lapchick was a Hall of Fame coach for the early New York Knicks.

Bernard King led the NBA by averaging 32.9 points per game in 1984–85. He is the only Knicks player ever to lead the league in scoring.

Basketball Association of America in 1946, the Knicks often have come close but have managed to win only two titles.

In the early days of the franchise, the Knicks advanced to the NBA Finals three consecutive years, only to come up short each time. They were led by Hall of Fame coach Joe Lapchick and All-Stars Carl Braun and Dick McGuire.

Then came a series of lean years until the arrival of center Willis Reed in 1964 and coach Red

Former Knicks forward Bill Bradley was a Rhodes scholar who went on to become a United States senator.

Bill Bradley drove from the Knicks to
the Hall of Fame and the U.S. Senate.

New York's Nat
"Sweetwater"
Clifton was the first
African-American
player to sign with
an NBA team.
The Knicks signed
the former Harlem
Globetrotters star
in 1950.

Holzman in 1967.
New York's 1969–70
team roared to 60
regular-season victo-
ries and the Eastern
Division title. That
team featured guards
Walt Frazier and Dick
Barnett, forwards
Dave DeBusschere
and Bill Bradley, and
Reed. After beating
Baltimore and
Milwaukee in the
playoffs, the Knicks outlasted Los Angeles in seven
games for their first NBA championship. New York
won 52, 48, and 57 games the next three seasons.
The Knicks won the league title again by downing
the Lakers in five games in the 1973 finals.

By the mid-1970s, the Knicks' run was over.
They had several losing seasons before bottoming
out with a last-place finish in 1984–85. Then came
the selection of Ewing. Though it took a few seasons, the club was back in the playoffs by 1987–88.

Willis Reed, known as the "Captain," combined inside strength and a soft touch to help the Knicks win two NBA titles.

The arrival of Patrick Ewing in 1985 was
a key turning point for the Knicks.

The name *Knicks* is short for knicker-bockers, the type of pants (knickers) that Dutch settlers in the area wore in the 1600s.

In 1969–70, Knicks center Willis Reed became the first player to earn MVP honors for the All-Star game, the regular season, and the NBA Finals in the same season.

Under coach Pat Riley from 1991–92 through 1994–95, New York posted 50 or more wins for four consecutive seasons and won two Atlantic Division titles. The 1994 team advanced to the finals before losing a seven-game heartbreaker to Houston. In 1999, the Knicks were the eighth and final seed in the East, but advanced all the way to the NBA Finals again. This time, they were **stymied** by San Antonio in five games.

Ewing's last season with the Knicks ended in 2000, when New York earned its 13th consecutive playoff berth. Prolific scorer Latrell Sprewell helped New York run its streak to 14 in 2000–01 before the club fell short of the postseason in 2001–02 and 2002–03.

THE ORLANDO MAGIC

Orlando's meteoric rise from expansion team to NBA finalist in its early years was downright, well . . . magical.

In 1987, owner Jim Hewitt was awarded a franchise for Orlando to begin play in the 1989–90 season. Former 76ers coach Matt Goukas was picked to lead the first Magic team, which included NBA veterans Reggie Theus and Terry Catledge and rookie Nick Anderson. Orlando only narrowly lost its first game to the Nets then beat the Knicks and the Cavaliers in its next two games. But the Magic went through an expansion team's typical growing pains, winning just 18 games its first year, 31 the next, and 21 the year after that.

Then a little bit of magic transformed the club overnight. Orlando drew the first pick in the lottery for the 1992 draft and used the choice to select imposing center Shaquille O'Neal from Louisiana State.

No one knew it at the time, but Orlando had

Illinois forward
Nick Anderson was
the Magic's first col-
lege draft selection
(in 1989). He spent
10 seasons with the
club and became its
all-time leading
scorer.

Orlando president Pat Williams was all smiles when his team chose Shaquille O'Neal in 1992.

become an instant playoff contender. The Magic improved their victory total by 20 games and finished 41–41 in 1992–93, missing the postseason only by a tiebreaker. O'Neal averaged 23.4 points and 13.9 rebounds and became the first rookie to start in the All-Star game since Michael Jordan in the mid-1980s.

Because Orlando was the best team in the league that didn't make the playoffs in 1992–93, the club had the worst chance of drawing the number-one slot in the 1993 draft lottery. But Orlando's 1-in-66 chance came up. The club would draft number one again.

Before he led the Lakers to three titles,
Shaq carried the Magic to the NBA Finals.

Hall of Famer Julius Erving joined the Magic front office as executive vice president in 1997.

This "Penny" is worth millions to the Magic.

Magic guard Scott Skiles dished out an NBA record 30 assists in a game against Denver in December 1990.

This time, the Magic selected Michigan forward Chris Webber and then promptly shipped him to the Warriors for guard Anfernee Hardaway. "Penny" was the perfect **complement** to the hulking O'Neal. And when Orlando added former Bulls forward Horace Grant to the mix the following year, the team was ready to make a run at the NBA championship.

Orlando's 1994–95 team won 57 games en route to its first Atlantic Division title. The Magic then beat Boston, Chicago, and Indiana in the playoffs to reach the NBA Finals in only its sixth season of existence.

Though the Rockets spoiled Orlando's title hopes, the Magic were now established on the scene. The departure of O'Neal to Los Angeles as a **free agent** in 1996 slowed Orlando's momentum, but the club found a new superstar in forward Tracy McGrady, who signed as a free agent in 2000. In 2002–03, McGrady was the league's leading scorer (at 32.1 points per game), but the Magic lost in the opening round of the playoffs.

Tracy "T-Mac" McGrady is one of the NBA's most exciting, high-scoring players.

THE PHILADELPHIA 76ERS

Some of the NBA's biggest stars have played for the 76ers franchise. They include Dolph Schayes in the club's early days; Wilt Chamberlain in the 1960s; Julius Erving in the 1970s and 1980s; and Allen Iverson since the 1990s. The wealth of individual talent has resulted in team success, too. Since joining the NBA in 1949–50, the club has won three league titles. Only the Celtics, Lakers, and Bulls have won more.

Actually, the club's first title came while the team played in Syracuse and was called the Nationals. Syracuse's roots went back to 1937. The club was one of six National Basketball League teams to survive the merger that resulted in the formation of the NBA in 1949.

At 6-foot-8, Schayes was one of the first big men who also had a **deft** shooting touch. With Schayes leading the way, the Nationals won 51 of 64 regular-season games. They advanced to the first NBA

Dolph Schayes (left) was one of the NBA's first all-around stars in the 1950s.

Finals before losing to Minneapolis. The Lakers foiled Syracuse's hopes again in 1954, but the Nationals won the 1955 title with a seven-game victory over Fort Wayne in the finals. In the last seconds of the decisive game, George King sank a free throw for a 92–91 lead and then stole the ball to preserve the victory.

The club relocated to Philadelphia for the 1963–64 season and was renamed the 76ers. Two years later, Philadelphia made big news by

Nationals owner Danny Biasone proposed a 24-second shot clock before the 1954–55 season. The clock revitalized the sport—and helped Syracuse overcome a 17-point deficit in the decisive game of the NBA Finals that season.

Wilt Chamberlain was a notoriously poor free-throw shooter who averaged only 51 percent for his career. But in his 100-point game while playing for the Warriors in 1962, he made 28 of his 32 free-throw tries.

Wilt Chamberlain scored in huge bunches, once averaging 50.4 points per game for a whole season!

acquiring 7-foot-1 center Wilt Chamberlain from the San Francisco Warriors. Chamberlain was a Philadelphia native who had begun playing for the Warriors in 1959, when the club was located in his hometown. In 1961–62, he averaged an unbelievable 50.4 points and 25.7 rebounds a game for the Warriors. Against New York that season, he scored a record 100 points in a game. He is still the only

Though only 6 foot, 1 inch (1.6 m), Allen Iverson
is one of the NBA's top scorers.

Hall of Famer
Billy Cunningham
played for the
NBA champion
76ers in 1966–67
and coached the
1982–83 team that
won the title.

player to reach that mark in an NBA game.

For all his prowess, the word on Chamberlain was that he couldn't win a championship. That changed in 1966–67. Teamed with fellow future Hall of Famers Hal Greer and Billy Cunningham, Chamberlain helped lead Philadelphia to a 68–13 record during the regular season. After ending Boston's eight-year run as NBA champions in the Eastern finals, the 76ers downed Chamberlain's old team, the Warriors, in six games to win the title.

Chamberlain played only one more year before being traded to Los Angeles, and the 76ers won only nine games in 1972–73. The club acquired its next big superstar in 1976, when Julius Erving was purchased from the New York Nets. "Dr. J" led the 76ers to the NBA Finals four times, the last of which resulted in a sweep of the Lakers for the 1983 championship.

Allen Iverson is the club's latest star. He's a prolific scorer who was the NBA's MVP in 2000–01, when he averaged 31.1 points per game and led the 76ers to the finals. Though Philadelphia lost to the Lakers, the 76ers have remained title contenders since.

THE WASHINGTON WIZARDS

Forgive the Washington Wizards if they suffer from a bit of an identity crisis. In a little more than 40 years of existence, they've played under six different names in three different cities.

The Wizards began as the Chicago Packers in 1961–62 and then changed their name to the Chicago Zephyrs the following season. Center Walt Bellamy, the top pick of the 1961 draft and a future Hall of Fame inductee, was the club's first star. But after two uneventful seasons in Chicago produced only 43 victories, a pair of last-place finishes, and few fans, the franchise moved to Baltimore and became known as the Bullets.

Things soon began looking up. In 1967, the club drafted guard Earl "the Pearl" Monroe from Winston-Salem State. The next year, the Bullets selected center Wes Unseld from the University of Louisville. Along with veterans such as high-flying forward Gus Johnson, the pieces were in place for

After starring for the Bullets, Earl "The Pearl" Monroe (15)
helped the Knicks win a pair of NBA titles.

Here's Bullets star Wes Unseld warming up before a game.

Former Bullets Dave Bing, Elvin Hayes, and Earl Monroe were all inducted into basketball's Hall of Fame in 1990. It's the only time that three members of the same franchise were inducted in the same year.

the most successful period in club history.

The stretch began when the Bullets had their first winning season, going 57–25 in 1968–69. It was the first of 10 winning seasons in 11 years and marked the start of 12 consecutive playoff appearances. Though the 1968–69 team was swept out of the playoffs by New York, the Bullets would reach the NBA Finals four times in the 1970s.

The highlight came in 1977–78, when the franchise won its lone NBA championship. By then, the team had moved to the nation's capital and was

The original Baltimore Bullets lasted from 1947–48 through 1953–54. That franchise won the 1947–48 league title, but it folded before the start of the 1954–55 season.

Elvin Hayes, "The Big E," was one of the best leapers and dunkers in NBA history.

known as the Washington Bullets (they were the Capital Bullets for one year), Monroe was playing for the Knicks, and Johnson had retired. Unseld, though, had been joined by 6-foot-11 forward Elvin Hayes, a first-round draft choice in 1972 who would go on to become the franchise's all-time leading scorer. After winning 44 games during the regular season, Washington eliminated Atlanta, San Antonio, and Philadelphia in the Eastern playoffs. Then they won a seven-game series over Seattle in the finals.

The SuperSonics avenged their loss to the Bullets in the 1979 finals, and since then, the

Bullets have had little success. From 1987–88 to 1995–96, Washington had nine consecutive losing seasons, including three last-place finishes. Before the 1997–98 season, the club changed its name to the Washington Wizards. Little changed on the court, however, and the club gradually declined until it won only 19 games in 2000–01.

The Wizards looked to Michael Jordan to bring some magic to D.C.

Not even the incomparable Michael Jordan could take the Wizards back to the playoffs in the early years of the new **millennium**. At 38, the former Bulls star came out of retirement to join the Wizards for the 2001–02 season. He led the team by averaging 22.9 points per game and helped Washington improve to 37 victories. But Washington won only 37 games again in 2002–03, narrowly missing the playoffs, and Jordan retired again.

Acrobatic forward Gus Johnson reputedly could leap high enough to touch the top of the backboard. He was one of the first players to make a driving slam dunk part of his repertoire.

TEAM RECORDS

TEAM	ALL-TIME RECORD	NBA TITLES (MOST RECENT)	NUMBER OF TIMES IN PLAYOFFS	TOP COACH (WINS)
BOSTON	2,656–1,773	16 (1985–86)	43	RED AUERBACH (795)
MIAMI	559–639	0	8	PAT RILEY (354)
NEW JERSEY	903–1,279	*2 (1975–76)	*19	KEVIN LOUGHERY (297)
NEW YORK	2,271–2,154	2 (1972–73)	37	RED HOLZMAN (613)
ORLANDO	567–549	0	8	BRIAN HILL (191)
PHILADELPHIA	2,312–1,942	3 (1982–83)	45	BILLY CUNNINGHAM (454)
WASHINGTON	1,560–1,841	1 (1977–78)	21	GENE SHUE (522)

*includes ABA

NBA ATLANTIC CAREER LEADERS (THROUGH 2002–03)

TEAM	CATEGORY	NAME (YEARS WITH TEAM)	TOTAL
BOSTON	POINTS	JOHN HAVLICEK (1962–1978)	26,395
	REBOUNDS	BILL RUSSELL (1956–1969)	21,620
MIAMI	POINTS	GLEN RICE (1989–95)	9,248
	REBOUNDS	RONY SEIKALY (1988–94)	4,544
NEW JERSEY	POINTS	BUCK WILLIAMS (1981–89)	10,440
	REBOUNDS	BUCK WILLIAMS (1981–89)	7,576
NEW YORK	POINTS	PATRICK EWING (1985–2000)	23,665
	REBOUNDS	PATRICK EWING (1985–2000)	10,759
ORLANDO	POINTS	NICK ANDERSON (1989–99)	10,650
	REBOUNDS	SHAQUILLE O'NEAL (1992–96)	3,691
PHILADELPHIA	POINTS	HAL GREER (1958–73)	21,586
	REBOUNDS	DOLPH SCHAYES (1949–64)	11,256
WASHINGTON	POINTS	ELVIN HAYES (1972–81)	15,551
	REBOUNDS	WES UNSELD (1968–81)	13,769

MEMBERS OF THE NAISMITH MEMORIAL NATIONAL BASKETBALL HALL OF FAME

BOSTON

PLAYER	POSITION	DATE INDUCTED
Nate Archibald	Guard	1991
Red Auerbach	Coach	1968
Dave Bing	Forward	1990
Larry Bird	Forward	1998
Walter Brown	Owner	1965
Bob Cousy	Guard	1970
Dave Cowens	Center	1991
John Havlicek	Forward	1983
Tom Heinsohn	Forward	1986
Bob Houbregs	Forward	1987
Bailey Howell	Guard	1997
K. C. Jones	Guard	1989
Sam Jones	Guard	1983
Alvin (Doggie) Julian	Coach	1967
Clyde Lovellette	Forward	1988
Ed Macauley	Center	1960
Pete Maravich	Guard	1987
Bob McAdoo	Center	2000
Kevin McHale	Forward	1999
Bill Mokray	Contributor	1965
Robert Parish	Center	2003
Andy Phillip	Guard	1961
Frank Ramsey	Guard	1981
Arnie Risen	Center	1998
Bill Russell	Center	1974
John (Honey) Russell	Coach	1964
Bill Sharman	Guard	1975
Bill Walton	Center	1993

NEW JERSEY

PLAYER	POSITION	DATE INDUCTED
Nate Archibald	Guard	1991
Rick Barry	Guard	1987
Lou Carnesecca	Coach	1992
Chuck Daly	Coach	1994
Julius Erving	Forward	1993
Bob McAdoo	Center	2000
Willis Reed	Center	1981

NEW YORK

PLAYER	POSITION	DATE INDUCTED
Walt Bellamy	Forward	1993
Bill Bradley	Forward	1982
Dave DeBusschere	Forward	1982
Walt Frazier	Guard	1987
Harry Gallatin	Guard	1991
Tom Gola	Center	1975
Red Holzman	Coach	1986
Joe Lapchick	Forward	1966
Jerry Lucas	Forward	1979
Slater Martin	Guard	1981
Bob McAdoo	Center	2000
Al McGuire	Guard	1992
Dick McGuire	Guard	1993
Earl Monroe	Guard	1990
Willis Reed	Center	1981

MEMBERS OF THE NAISMITH MEMORIAL NATIONAL BASKETBALL HALL OF FAME

PHILADELPHIA

PLAYER	POSITION	DATE INDUCTED
Al Cervi	Guard	1984
Wilt Chamberlain	Center	1978
Billy Cunningham	Forward	1986
Julius Erving	Forward	1993
Hal Greer	Guard	1981
Alex Hannum	Forward	1998
Bailey Howell	Forward	1997
Earl Lloyd	Forward	2003
Moses Malone	Center	2001
Bob McAdoo	Center	2000
Jack Ramsay	Coach	1992
Dolph Schayes	Forward	1972
George Yardley	Forward	1996

WASHINGTON

PLAYER	POSITION	DATE INDUCTED
Walt Bellamy	Guard	1993
Dave Bing	Forward	1990
Alex Hannum	Coach	1998
Elvin Hayes	Center	1990
Bailey Howell	Forward	1997
Harry Jeannette	Guard	1994
K. C. Jones	Guard	1989
Moses Malone	Center	2001
Earl Monroe	Guard	1990
Jim Pollard	Forward	1977
Wes Unseld	Center	1988

Note: Orlando and Miami do not have any members in the Hall of Fame (yet!).

**Three Hall of Famers: Philadelphia's Moses Malone,
Billy Cunningham, and Julius Erving.**

GLOSSARY

armory—a building for housing military equipment or personnel

complement—one part that makes another part or parts whole

deft—skillful

defunct—no longer active; closed down

flagship—the most notable of a particular group

free agent—an athlete who has finished his contract with one team and is eligible to sign with another

inauspicious—not successful or fortunate

millennium—a span of 1,000 years; in this case, the period beginning in 2000

nadir—the lowest point

NBA Finals—a seven-game series between the winners of the NBA's Eastern and Western Conference championships

nomadic—wandering in search of a permanent place

playoffs—a four-level postseason elimination tournament involving eight teams from each conference; levels include two rounds of divisional playoffs (best of five games and best of seven), a conference championship round (best of seven), and the NBA Finals (best of seven)

regular-season—describes an 82-game schedule in which each of the NBA's 29 teams plays 54 games within its conference, 24 of which are within its division; a team plays two games against each team outside its conference, one at home and one away

semipros—short for semiprofessionals, this term describes individuals who play a sport for money or some sort of gain, but who don't view playing the sport as their full-time occupation

sixth man—a basketball team's key substitute, the first player off the bench after the starting five

stymied—blocked

TIME LINE

1946 The Boston Celtics and the New York Knicks begin play as charter members of the BAA (the forerunner to the NBA)

1949 The Syracuse Nationals make their NBA debut

1957 Boston wins its first NBA title

1959 The Celtics win the first of a record eight consecutive league championships

1961 The Chicago Packers join the NBA

1963 The Chicago Zephyrs (formerly the Packers) move to Baltimore and become the Bullets

1963 The Nationals move from Syracuse to Philadelphia and become the 76ers

1967 The 76ers win the NBA title and stop Boston's string of eight consecutive championships

1967 The New Jersey Americans (now the Nets) begin play as charter members of the ABA

1970 The Knicks win their first NBA title

1973 The Baltimore Bullets move to Washington and become the Capital Bullets (later the Washington Bullets and now the Washington Wizards)

1974 The Nets win the first of two ABA titles in three seasons

1978 Washington wins its lone NBA championship

1988 Miami begins play as an expansion team

1989 Orlando begins play as an expansion team

1994 Orlando reaches the NBA Finals in only its sixth season

2003 New Jersey reaches its second consecutive NBA Finals

FOR MORE INFORMATION ABOUT THE ATLANTIC DIVISION AND THE NBA

BOOKS

Grabowski, John F. *The Boston Celtics*. San Diego: Lucent Books, 2002.

Macht, Norman L. *Julius Erving*. Broomall, Pa.: Chelsea House Publishers, 1994.

Miller, Ray. *Michael Jordan*. San Diego: Kidhaven, 2002.

Schultz, Randy. *The New York Knicks Basketball Team*. Berkeley Heights, N.J.: Enslow Publishers, 2000.

ON THE WEB

Visit our home page for lots of links about Atlantic Division teams:

http://www.childsworld.com/links.html

NOTE TO PARENTS, TEACHERS, AND LIBRARIANS: We routinely check our Web links to make sure they're safe, active sites—so encourage your readers to check them out!

INDEX

A B O U T   T H E   A U T H O R

Jim Gigliotti is a former editor at the National Football League who now is a freelance writer based in southern California. His recent writing credits include *Baseball: A Celebration* (with James Buckley Jr.) and several children's books on NASCAR history and personalities.